TIDDLES

The Special
Tassie Devil

by

Nita Lawes-Gilvear

Illustrations by

Leighton Lee

When Mrs Tassie Devil decided to move to a cave near the Greenfields farm not far from a town called Devonport in Tasmania, she did not realise that town life would be so different for her two young Devils. She had always been used to the ways of the wilderness, where people rarely came near the dens and the young Devils would only know the tiger cats and wombats as their neighbours.

She thought life would be easier away from the harshness of the bush where animals had to fight for their food to survive. She knew there was a lot of food to be had near the farms where most people lived. Her two youngsters, Dozer and Tiddles found other interests.

Tiddles was very interested in Katie's yellow teddy bear. Katie lived at the farm near their cave. Tiddles asked her mother if she could have one like it.

"No you can't!" said her mother. "Tassie Devils do not have teddy bears."

Baby Tiddles was very angry and stamped her little feet on the stone floor. "I want a teddy bear like Katie's!"

"The only thing you will get is yourself into trouble if you're going to be naughty," said her mother.

"You are a nasty, mean mother," said Tiddles. "You don't love me. I'm going to run away and then you'll be sorry."

Katie and Sammie, the black sheep dog, were running along a pathway near the Mersey River that ran through their farm. They were both very excited because Mrs Tassie Devil had moved in from the bush near the Western Tiers.

Nearing the cave, they walked very carefully under the golden wattle blossom trees. Tasmanian Devils sleep all day and they do not welcome visitors. They heard a strange noise.

"It sounds like an animal crying," Katie said. Sammie was the only one who knew Katie could talk to the animals.

Katie and Sammie looked toward the river and just could not believe their eyes. Beside a small rock sat a little Tasmanian Devil. Teardrops ran down her little face and splashed onto her feet. Katie ran forward to see what was the matter with her.

"Oh dear me," said Katie, "whatever is making you so unhappy?"

"My mother calls me Baby Tiddles and I'm NOT a baby," said the little Tasmanian Devil. "My brother Dozer is mean and very bad tempered. He steals my food and pushes me off our straw bed onto the cold floor. Dozer said if I got into the bed again he would bite the end off my tail."

"Oh dear me," said Sammie, "this is a serious problem. I'd better go and speak to your mother."

"Oh no, PLEASE don't do that. She's been hunting for food all night and travelled all the way to Trowunna Wildlife Park to visit our cousins. If you wake her up she might bite your head off."

"Don't you cry any more," said Katie, "we will get you some food."

Katie and Sammie ran back home to get some raw meat and a little sheep skin mat for her to sleep on. Katie pulled a little red knitted hat out of her pocket and put it on Tiddles' head to keep her ears warm. While Tiddles was eating the meat Katie noticed the white shaped star on the shoulder which stood out very clearly against her black coat.

"I wonder what it means?" asked Sammie.

"Something very special I would think," said Katie.

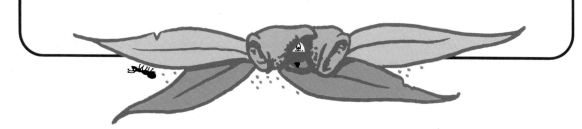

Baby Tiddles was not going home until she could do something special. As she watched the birds flying she thought it would be good if she learned to fly. That would be something VERY special.

She climbed to the top of a big rock and jumped off, trying to flap her legs sideways like the wings of a bird. This was a terrible disaster.

Tiddles dropped like a stone and landed in a crumpled heap at the bottom of the rock.

On his way home from the sheep paddock, Sammie found Baby Tiddles. "Oh my stars, whatever happened to you, Tiddles?"
The baby Devil was making strange noises as if she was having a bad dream. Sammie woke her up. "Whatever is the matter with you, Tiddles?"

"I was trying to fly because I wanted to do something special and visit my cousins on Cradle Mountain," she said. "then I had a terrible dream. Big black ants on pink roller skates were running over my poor sore head."

Katie and Sammie visited Tiddles every day because she was lonely. Sammie brought her meat and Katie told her all about the big ship named the Spirit of Tasmania that comes to Devonport, bringing people from all over the world. Many tourists who have travelled around Tasmania called the State 'Paradise Island'.

Every year there was a teddy bears' picnic at Greenfields near the river. All Katie's school friends came with their teddy bears and their parents. On the day of the teddy bears' picnic there was great excitement. Katie and Sammie had planned a big surprise for everyone.

A coach load of tourists had just arrived when they saw Katie and Sammie. They stopped and stared. Katie was pulling along a little red cart and there was Baby Tiddles sitting up, hugging a yellow teddy bear with the red knitted hat pulled over her ears.

All the visitors rushed forward to take Tiddles' photo and some had movie cameras. Katie knew the white star on Tiddles' shoulder had meant something special after all. Baby Tiddles was very happy as she was a film star and the main attraction at the teddy bears' picnic.

Baby Tiddles picked up her sheep skin mat and hurried home to her mother. She curled up on the mat with the little teddy bear Katie had given her. The last thought Tiddles had as she drifted off to sleep was there was no place like home after all. Her mother gave a big sigh as she lay beside Tiddles. That was one lesson she had learned, that things near the towns were very different from the bush. Whoever heard of a Tasmanian Devil having a teddy bear? Whoever heard of one sleeping on a sheep skin mat? They would not believe her the next time she went to the Trowunna Wildlife Park.

The End